Ava and the "Monsters"

by
Phillip D. Cortez

Illustrated by
Carizza Bognot Losbaños

1580 Publishing

ISBN: 978-0-9964623-3-4

www.phillipcortez.com

@phillipdcortez

Photography: Christ Chavez - www.christchavez.com

For Papa Honey & his "Little General..."
For Patty & our "Little Monsters"
- PDC

For my family, Merlin, Mia and my parents.
- CBL

Ava lay on her bed, staring at the ceiling in her bedroom while the rest of the children in her neighborhood played outside. Though the screams of laughter and fun could be heard just outside her window, she felt like she was a world away, stuck inside like a caged bird surrounded by boredom. The ceiling looked like it had been sprayed with popcorn, forming different shapes and patterns. She would try and form different objects within those patterns, a poor substitute for the animals and dragons she'd normally see in the puffy clouds scattered across the blue sky outside. Outside is where she really wanted to be.

"What am I going to do now?" she sighed.

She wasn't used to being in trouble, especially at home. Sure, there were those times when she felt like pulling out every strand of her little sister Zoe's hair when she acted like a brat, which happened often. But for the most part, Ava was good about remembering that Zoe was just a chatty three-year-old that wanted to be just like her big sister.

Ava wasn't penned up in her room for fighting with Zoe, though. She was grounded because of an incident that happened at school, a disagreement between Ava and her fourth grade teacher, Mr. Marley (all the kids in school called him Mr. Gnarly).

"Ava, I don't know what it is you're looking at outside the window but it'd be wise on your part to pay attention," Mr. Marley announced. "Honestly, I don't know where your mind goes."

The rest of the children in class snickered and giggled. They called her "Far Away Ava" because she liked talking about dragons and superheroes and far away places where little girls like her could fly.

And who could blame her? She was excited at the idea of going to school every day and learning. But each new day was the same old thing, especially in Mr. Marley's class. If he wasn't bragging about that garden of his and his prized squash, he was gloating over his "perfect" dog, Buster (little did he know that the mutt roamed the neighborhood like a small bully, digging up flower beds and knocking over trash cans).

So when Mr. Marley wondered where Ava's mind went, she decided to answer him – out loud for the entire class to hear:

"My mind goes anywhere and everywhere, any place and any time away from here," she announced bravely.

And for that, Ava was sent to the office, where she was given a week of after school detention for talking back to her teacher, the very boring Mr. Marley.

This was why Ava found herself in trouble, sent to her room while all the kids in the neighborhood were outside having fun.

It's why she was so bored, trying to make shapes out of ceiling popcorn instead of puffy clouds.

The next day after the final bell rang, Ava headed to the library for detention. Part of her punishment was to help straighten out the books, make sure they were in order and help Mrs. Pennywise, the school librarian, with anything else she might need.

"Ava, will you help me find some good Halloween web sites online?" Mrs. Pennywise asked. "I'd like to try and get some good decorating ideas for the Fall Festival next month."

The school's annual Fall Festival was over a month away but the planning committee, led by Mrs. Pennywise, was full speed ahead on all the preparations.

"What's the theme going to be this year?" Ava asked.

"That's a good question," Mrs. Pennywise said as she piled a stack of colorful books next to her computer. One by one she carefully inspected the pages and made sure they weren't torn or dog-eared or marked on.

"It seems like all the kids these days are into comic book characters. I think it's fine time we bring back good old fashioned monsters."

Monsters? Ava wondered. Mrs.
Pennywise must have seen the
confused look on Ava's face, so she
continued.

"You might be too young to
remember but a long time ago
when I was a little girl we used
to be afraid of monsters like
The Wolf Man, Frankenstein's
Creature, the Mad Scientist
or the Mummy. We want
you kids to be creative and
original with your costumes
for the Fall Festival."

"No store costumes will be
allowed; students must make
their own costumes."

Ava didn't think about monsters on the way home from school that afternoon. A slight breeze carrying the smell of someone grilling burgers in a backyard somewhere filled the air. Even in early September Ava noticed the last signs of summer still trying to hold on before Fall took over and turned the skies grey.

She walked down the sidewalk until it came to an end and became a dirt path. New homes were being built throughout the neighborhood. Ava thought they looked like wooden skeletons. She wondered who'd eventually move into these new homes, whether there'd be kids her own age living inside and, more importantly, she wondered if any of them would be her friends.

She remembered when the tractors and dump trucks first arrived, clearing out the desert land to make room for all of the construction work required to build these new homes. Ava would hear the pounding of hammers and screaming saws mixed with the sound of old music coming from an AM radio station. Sometimes the construction workers sang along to the static-filled music. The days, weeks and months that followed were a combination of singing, laughter and the smell of saw dust as the new homes changed the neighborhood landscape forever.

Yes, her little town of Horizon was getting bigger. This small exit on the map near El Paso, Texas was growing like the yellow poppies at the foot of the Franklin Mountains. During the day, especially on her walk home from school, Ava's mind could drift free without kids making fun of her, where she could look at the prickly desert dunes and imagine they were baby dinosaurs with spiky backs.

And at night she could sit up on her rock wall and look up at the stars with her father. She'd hear his stories about how each star was a sun for a different system of planets. They talked about the possibility of other forms of life in outer space and he'd encourage her to imagine what some aliens might look like. Ava's father loved it when she used her imagination.

A few days later, on her way home from helping Mrs. Pennywise in the library, Ava saw something even she could never imagine. Something moved out of the corner of her eye.

She uttered the words "Who's there?" but she couldn't hear the sound of her own voice. In the distance, just past one of the half-built houses, was a moving yucca plant, swaying in the sun yet there was no breeze outside.

She could have sworn she saw something. Or was it her imagination? With all of this talk about the Fall Festival and monsters and costumes, was her imagination getting the best of her?

So she kept walking. Her big brown eyes focused on the narrow dirt path in front of her until the flap of a bird's wings startled her. The bird rested on top of another yucca, only this one a bit bigger than the rest of them. Ava kept her eye on the bird – actually, the bird looked like it had kept an eye on Ava – and she noticed a shiny hint of crimson on its breast in the shimmering sun.

The bird flew away just as quickly as it had landed and Ava watched it fly off into the horizon until it blended into the blue sky. That's when Ava saw what looked to be a sea of yuccas, even more than before. The desert was filled with them as far as her big brown eyes could see. They seemed to be moving, in unison, as if swaying to a song.

She took a careful step with her left foot and as she began to move forward Ava heard what sounded like a rattle coming from one of the yuccas. She turned towards the noise and saw that the sound was coming from a yucca standing no more than 10 feet from her. The base of the bush looked like a pineapple and shook like a maraca.

Am I imagining this? Ava thought. "Yes, I must be imagining this," she quietly answered herself.

The rattling sound grew stronger. The ground shook at the pineapple base of the yucca followed by the sound of snapping roots and the smell of West Texas dirt. She stood there, frozen as if her feet had roots of their own.

She watched in disbelief as a tiny plant-like creature emerged from the ground. A pair of huge eyes blinked at her, as if the creature was just as startled as Ava was.

And before Ava could say a word, the tiny creature went back inside the ground and blended with all the desert yucca bushes.

Days went by. And even though she no longer had to stay for after school detention, she stayed in the library anyway. She enjoyed talking to Mrs. Pennywise, helping her put books away and hearing about the latest plans for the big Fall Festival. But really all Ava wanted to do was see that desert creature again. So far there was no sign of it.

She thought about those huge round eyes staring at her. And her mind drifted towards that afternoon, how the bird with the crimson chest startled her and how the yucca plant rattled. Was there more than one of them? Were they nice creatures? Ava's mind was full of questions.

"If only I could see the creature again," Ava sighed.

"What was that, Ava?" asked Mrs. Pennywise.
"What's this about a creature?"

"Oh, it's something I'm thinking about for my
Halloween costume," Ava nervously replied. "It's kind
of like a desert cactus creature."

"That's brilliant!" Mrs. Pennywise exclaimed. "That's
the most original costume idea I've heard yet. I can't
wait to see what you come up with!"

It actually would make for a pretty good costume,
Ava thought. But Ava hoped she wasn't just
imagining things, that she really did see something
in the desert that day, that her head wasn't in the
clouds.

Far away.

The sun was hidden behind grey clouds on her way home from school that afternoon. Soon the time would change, as the days seemed to be getting shorter. At first the sudden gust of wind sounded like a passing car but when Ava turned to look there was nothing there. Just the clown bushes, she thought, referring to the round bushes and weeds that looked like green and yellow clown wigs that had been thrown all over the ground.

That's when she heard a voice.

"Anywhere and everywhere, any place and any time away from here," said the voice with a chuckle.

"Who's there?" Ava asked.

And with that, one of the round, green bushes rolled its way to her feet. With a short grunt, this green desert creature stretched out a pair of arms, legs and let out a happy hello.

"Don't you just love this weather?" the talking bush asked.

"Who..what...are you?" Ava began.

"Pardon my manners, miss, we certainly do not mean to frighten you," the green bush said.

"Did you say 'We?' How many of you are there?" Ava curiously asked.

Ava could hardly contain the excitement she felt in seeing this talking bush-like creature one more time. She wasn't frightened at all, even though she probably should have been. But somehow Ava knew that this little creature was friendly.

The bush creature went on to explain that they were a species called the Wakala. The Wakala lived deep inside the natural world, ever so close to humans, yet at the same time so very far away. They could be found in trees, bushes, plants and forests, as well as jungles, swamps and marshes throughout the world.

"If you were to see what we really looked like it would frighten you," the creature said. "So we take on the form of our natural surroundings, including the Yucca plant, small bushes and cacti. You can call me Wally."

"Wally the Wakala!" Ava laughed. "My name is Ava! Will you be my friend?"

"We thought you'd never ask! We've been watching you and have admired your imagination and wonder for a long time. You see, Ava, you have the tremendous gift of letting your imagination take off like a rocket ship exploring new worlds."

Ava smiled. "Anywhere and everywhere," she said.

"That's right," agreed Wally. "Your imagination is what takes you to any place and any time – "

"Away from here," Ava interrupted.

And with that, Wally closed his eyes and rolled into a round, green desert bush.

"Until next time!" Wally assured her.

Ava took another long, deep breath of the moist desert air and hurried home.

On her way she looked around and saw desert hills, bushes, cacti and yucca plants scattered throughout the landscape. And she knew that from this day forward, she'd never see them the same again.

Ava didn't spend as much time with Mrs. Pennywise in the library over the next few weeks. Instead, she'd hurry home after the final bell, change clothes and go play in the desert while she still had daylight. While most people saw thorny patches of desert hills, Ava saw the perfect fort; all she needed was one of her father's shovels to tunnel through and dig trenches, using any piece of scrap material left behind by the homebuilders.

And, of course, there was Wally, who'd introduced Ava to other Wakala friends of his own. Together they made their desert forts, a small network of bunkers and tunnels. It was the perfect place to let her imagination run wild. And although there were too many Wakalas to count, Ava got along with all of them. But there was something Ava kept thinking about, something that bothered her.

The next afternoon, as Ava and her desert friends continued to make their very own fortresses, she stopped and approached Wally.

"Wally?" Ava began. He could see that there was something bothering her. All of the Wakala did. They, too, stopped what they were doing to listen.

"What do you really look like?" she asked.

"My dear, should that matter at all to you?" Wally replied.

Ava thought about Wally's question. Maybe it didn't matter what Wally and his Wakala friends looked like.

"Hiding is the only way the Wakala get to share the outside world with people," Wally said. "It helps us blend in."

Ava thought for a moment. Wally had talked about how the Wakala would be too scary to see for humans.

"But you get to see me as I really am," Ava finally said. "And if you're as nice as a Wakala as you are a round, green desert bush, how could I be frightened of you?"

"Ava, this is why you are so special," Wally said. The rest of the Wakala nodded in agreement. "Along with that curiosity and imagination of yours is a big heart."

"There are a lot more people like me," Ava replied. "Maybe if you gave more of us a chance?"

"We're taking a chance on you, Ava," Wally said.
"When the time is right perhaps I'll show you what a
Wakala really looks like."

It's not fair. This was the thought that swam inside of Ava's head like a goldfish circling a tiny clear bowl. For almost a month she had found friends to play and imagine with. Not like the kids that laughed at her at school, especially in Mr. Marley's class. She didn't think it was fair that she had to play with her new friends, her far away friends, in secret.

Wally was right about Ava, though. She was as curious a girl as the rest of the Wakala were, who decided to blend in with nature in order to enjoy the light of day – and share the outside world with the humans that unknowingly shared the planet with them.

But Wally was also right about the size of Ava's heart. The more she thought about the whole situation, the more she began to truly feel bad for Wally and his friends. The Wakala had a history of its own, a history unknown to the rest of the human world, at least. Having to hide and remain a secret must have been terrible for them.

Suddenly Ava felt guilty for thinking that it wasn't fair for her when it really wasn't fair for the Wakala.

"There has to be a way we can play together without having to hide from the rest of the world," she yawned.

That sweet smell of desert moisture gently breezed through her open window and Ava turned to close it just in case raindrops began to fall. Her room was dark except for the glow of the moon peeking through her window. Even as her eyelids grew heavy under thick lashes and sleepiness, she noticed that it was a bigger moon than usual (She thought it looked like a buttery pancake). It was a perfect moon for fall. And as she began to fade into a long sleep, Ava suddenly sat up in her bed.

She had a bright idea.

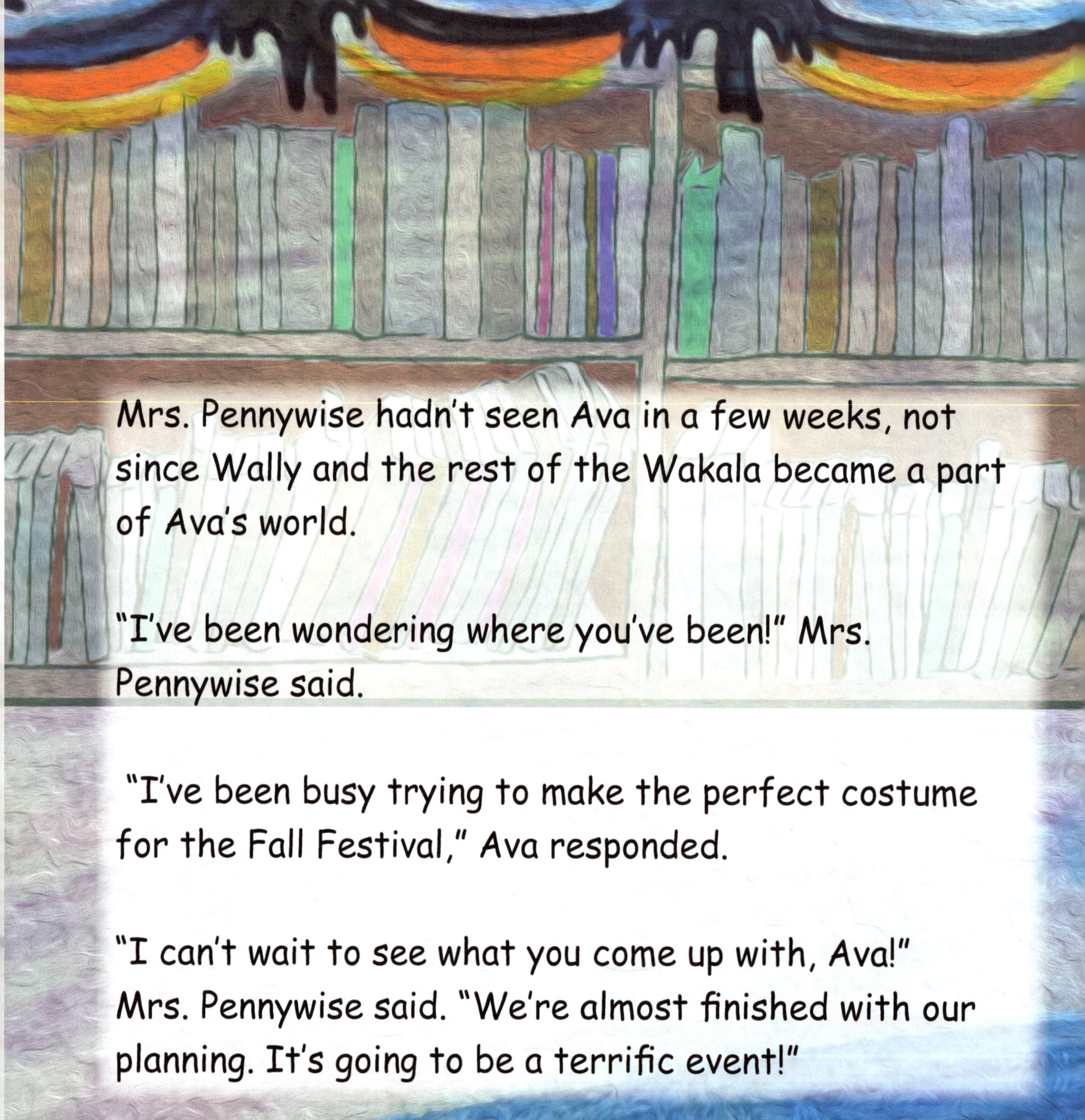

Mrs. Pennywise hadn't seen Ava in a few weeks, not since Wally and the rest of the Wakala became a part of Ava's world.

"I've been wondering where you've been!" Mrs. Pennywise said.

"I've been busy trying to make the perfect costume for the Fall Festival," Ava responded.

"I can't wait to see what you come up with, Ava!" Mrs. Pennywise said. "We're almost finished with our planning. It's going to be a terrific event!"

"Mrs. Pennywise?" Ava began. She was a little nervous, as Ava's entire plan hinged on Mrs. Pennywise's response.

"What's wrong dear?" Mrs. Pennywise asked. She could see that there was something on Ava's mind. "Is everything ok?"

"Everything's fine," Ava replied. "I was just wondering if I could bring some friends to the Fall Festival."

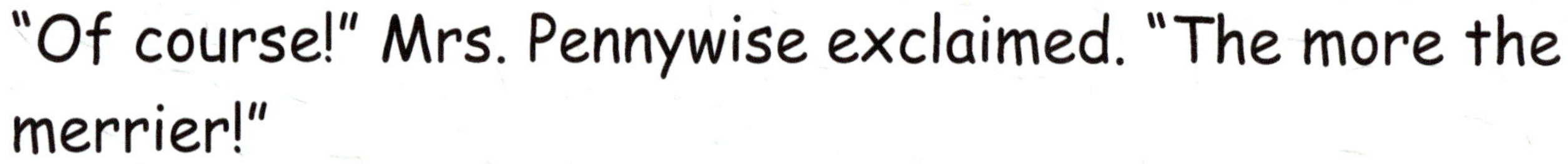

"Of course!" Mrs. Pennywise exclaimed. "The more the merrier!"

"There's something else I wanted to ask you, Mrs. Pennywise," Ava said.

Ava went on to explain that she had made friends from another school and that they had started a band.

"I'll bet you want to know whether it's ok for your band to play at the festival, right?" the librarian asked.

"That's exactly what I wanted to ask you," Ava smiled.

"That sounds terrific! What do you call yourselves?" Mrs. Pennywise asked.

Ava hadn't really thought about a name for the group. So she said the first thing that popped into her mind.

"We go by Ava and the Monsters," she replied. "We play in our costumes."

"That's brilliant!" Mrs. Pennywise shouted.

Ava smiled, gathered her backpack and began to leave the library. She nearly walked through the door when Mrs. Pennywise stopped her.

"Ava," she said. "I can't wait to hear you play!"

Ava smiled and walked home under a blue and purple sky filled with wispy clouds that looked like they were painted with a brush. Her plan was now set in motion. Because if there was one day out of the year where people could dress up like anything they wanted, it was Halloween.

Now all she had to do was convince Wally and the rest of the Wakala to participate.

"There's only one tiny detail you've left out," said Wally the next afternoon at their secret desert fort. The rest of the Wakala had listened to Ava explain her plan and were now curious to hear what Wally had to say.

"First of all, we do not play instruments," Wally said. "A band has to play music."

"Our voices can be our instruments," Ava replied. "All we have to do is just show up and sing."

"In costumes, you mean?" Wally asked.

"Well, yes, I'll dress up as a desert plant creature and we can go together," Ava said. "It's the perfect plan."

"Actually it's not quite perfect," Wally replied.

"What do you mean, Wally? I dress up like a plant creature and we get to hang out together in front of other people without a care in the world. Nobody would even notice because it'd be Halloween. That's when everyone dresses up like something different."

"But we'd still be hiding," Wally replied. "Remember when you asked to see what I really looked like? I've been thinking about what you said and I think the time is finally right to venture out into the daylight as our real selves."

Ava knew that Wally was right. She thought it was funny that humans hid behind masks for only one night out of the year - and the Wakala did it all year long. Now, at the Fall Festival, it'd be the opposite. The humans would hide while the Wakala could finally be themselves.

"You're right, Wally. My plan will only work if I dress up like the real you: as a Wakala."

"But that means..."

"That means, "Ava interrupted, "that you must take off your costume and show your true self."

Ava paused and saw that Wally was nervous.

"Starting right now," she said.

A fresh, fall breeze whipped through the air as Wally let out a deep breath. The sky above was a deep blue yet the setting sun colored the horizon an array of oranges and purples and pinks. The breeze shook the desert bushes like maracas and a cloud of dust kicked up around Wally as he began to spin around like a toy top moving faster and faster.

Ava stepped away as did the rest of the Wakala to give Wally room. He spun faster and faster until he became a blur. She could only make out the shape of him in the middle of what looked like a dust devil, a small tornado of desert dust. She squinted her eyes but the blowing sand forced Ava to turn her head away. When Wally finally stopped she opened her eyes and saw what no human being ever saw before: a real Wakala.

Wally was no longer a desert bush-like creature. Instead, Ava stared face to face with a strange being the color of licorice with a screw-like head for tunneling underground and four legs that looked like thick roots with shovel blades at each end.

"Are you frightened?" he asked.

"This is you!" she shouted!

"This is me," Wally said. "Please do not be scared."

"Scared? You're, like, the coolest creature I've ever seen! This is going to be so awesome!"

Wally and the rest of the Wakala let out a blast of approval, a sound that filled the air and reminded Ava of trombones and trumpets.

"That's the sound we make when we're happy!" Wally exclaimed.

"So you DO play an instrument!" Ava screamed.

Ava, Wally and the rest of the Wakala met every day after school, practicing their performance until the time had finally arrived for them to put her plan in motion – the school's Fall Festival.

No sooner had Ava and her Wakala friends arrived at the Fall Festival that a small crowd of people gathered around them. Kids, grown-ups and especially Mrs. Pennywise thought that Ava and her friends looked good enough to be in a movie. Even Mr. Marley was impressed.

"Terrific costumes!" said a group of older kids. "Where'd you get that idea from?" one of the parents asked.

"It was his idea," Ava replied, turning her attention to Wally. She thought he looked a bit nervous. After all, this was his first encounter with other people as a true Wakala.

"We should go hang out back stage and wait until it's our turn to go on."

"Good idea," Wally said.

"Guys, let me be the first to introduce you to the wonderful experience of cotton candy!" Ava announced to the small group of Wakala.

Ava bought four puffs of cotton candy and brought them back stage to Wally and the gang. Each looked slightly puzzled.

"You let it melt in your mouth," Ava instructed. She then tore off a pink piece of cotton candy and placed it on her tongue.

"Like this?" Wally asked, and with one snort he vacuumed the entire puff of cotton candy into his mouth.

"Ahhh! That was delicious!" he exclaimed.

The rest of the Wakala followed suit. Each of them loved their cotton candy.

"I can eat this forever!" one of the Wakala said.

"You guys love cotton candy as much as I do," Ava smiled. "It's almost time to go on. Is everyone ready?"

"Ava, we've been ready to do this for a very long time," Wally said. "Thank you."

Ava smiled at her friend. She wanted to thank him, too. After all, Wally could have chosen any other boy or girl to befriend. Just then, Mrs. Pennywise peaked at Ava from in front of the curtain to let her know that it was time to go on.

Ava turned to her friends and smiled. "Anywhere and everywhere, any place and any time," she began. "There's no other place I'd rather be than here with you!"

When the curtain opened Ava took her drum. Two bangs followed the stomp of her foot. She repeated the beat until the crowd began to do the same. Meanwhile the Wakala shuffled on stage to the beat, making happy horn sounds.

"We're 'Ava and the Monsters' and the name of this song is called **The Wakala Stomp!**"

Ava then sang into the microphone:

ANYWHERE AND EVERYWHERE
ANY TIME AND ANY PLACE
THERE ARE CREATURES ALL AROUND
AND THEY HAVE A FUNNY FACE

DO THE STOMP! (Bing-Bang STOMP! Bing-Bang STOMP!)
DO THE WAKALA STOMP! (Bing-Bang STOMP! Bing-Bang STOMP!)

THEY DON'T LOOK LIKE ME AND YOU
BUT THEY'RE FRIENDLY AS CAN BE
ALL THEY NEED IS A CHANCE
GIVE THEM TIME, YOU'LL SEE

DO THE STOMP! (Bing-Bang STOMP! Bing-Bang STOMP!)
DO THE WAKALA STOMP! (Bing-Bang STOMP! Bing-Bang STOMP!)

THEY COME FROM UNDERGROUND
THEY'RE AS CURIOUS AS CAN BE
ALL THEY NEEDED WAS A FRIEND
SO THEY TOOK A CHANCE ON ME

DO THE STOMP! (Bing-Bang STOMP! Bing-Bang STOMP!)
DO THE WAKALA STOMP! (Bing-Bang STOMP! Bing-Bang STOMP!)

IF YOU SEE SOMEONE WHO'S DIFFERENT
SHARE THIS SONG FROM ME TO YOU
ALL THEY NEED IS A FRIEND
WHO KNOWS? THAT COULD BE YOU!

DO THE STOMP! (Bing-Bang STOMP! Bing-Bang STOMP!)
DO THE WAKALA STOMP! (Bing-Bang STOMP! Bing-Bang STOMP!)

The End.
(Or the beginning).

Phillip D. Cortez

The story of Ava and the Monsters literally began the day Phillip's daughter, Ava, saw a Halloween mask in her older brother's room.

"She couldn't get over the sight of that mask," Cortez said. "My wife and I were afraid it was going to creep her out but instead Ava was totally into it. From that point on, all she wanted to talk about were monsters. Her imagination took over from there. Today it's all about dragons and superheroes."

Ava and the Monsters is Cortez's third children's book, a project that wasn't originally on his radar.

Ava Cortez

"I was supposed to be finishing up a collection of short stories and essays, which I'll get to, but the more I listened to her play with her sister, cousins and even by herself, she was always talking to and about monsters. So I came up with a concept and shared it with the kids I was speaking to at local schools while promoting my second book. The kids loved the concept and played a big part in helping me brainstorm some ideas. This was really an organic project that basically started out with a kid's imagination and contributed to by other kids throughout El Paso. I just sort of put the pieces together."

On working with Carizza Bognot Losbaños

"There was a simplicity yet a very captivating style that I noticed about her work when I first encountered it. And since the main character of this story is a littler girl, I thought it only made sense that the art was created by an artist who could innately bring those feminine qualities to life. I couldn't have been happier working with Carizza on this project."

Phillip D. Cortez lives and works in El Paso, Texas with his wife (and patient editor), Patty and their four monsters: Ivan, Cameron, Ava and Zoe.

Carizza Bognot Losbaños

There's always a story behind every illustration. Carizza Bognot Losbaños' art reflects fun- filled memories of childhood with her playful use of vivid hues and subjects close to the child in everyone. Combined with surrealism, her paintings of acrylic show appeal to young and mature individuals alike.

Carizza was born on November 13, 1984 and grew up in Quezon City. She graduated with a degree of Bachelor of Fine Arts Major in Advertising from the University of Santo Tomas. Her family had a thriving sewing machine business and her parents wanted her to take up a business course instead. Still, Carizza pursued her passion for art without hesitation. Her efforts and creativity won her the best thesis in 2004. This thesis of a storybook illustration of Pure Magic, a story about believing in possibilities, was recognized for its vibrantly colorful acrylic backgrounds.

Not the only artist in the family, Carizza's grandfather had been a pianist soloing for the regal Imelda Marcos, and her father occasionally made sketches. This impressionable artist started as an art teacher in Art Attack and taught children ages 2 to 10. Utilizing her inherent abilities in her line of work, she developed an advertising career, working as a graphic artist, creative head, corporate designer.

Her fun- loving spirit and childlike nature are attributes evident in her works. Her cartoonistic characters donning tiny blouses and skirts are undoubtedly an influence of elementary and high school life at St. Theresa's College. Carizza's primary inspiration is her two- year old daughter, Mia. The many influences in her life had truly contributed to her current style.

For Carizza, like the child in each one of us, the dream of believing should also live on. Dream more, Do More are her words of inspiration for young artists like her. To inspire youth, especially mothers, to persist in their efforts to leave a lasting legacy to their successors, is her long- term goal. Certainly, the much adored qualities of children and the youthful vigor in her paintings give onlookers a refreshingly new perspective of the arts.